SEE YOU LATER
CROC-A-GATOR

ISHELTON BOOKS

WRITTEN BY IMOGEN SHELTON   ILLUSTRATED BY ALINA KRALIA

For my husband, my children, Jack and Ben,
and my friends and family all over the globe.

Time and distance have no effect on the love I have for each of you.

Published in the United States by IShelton Books LLC
For more information about this book visit our website/contact:
www.isheltonbooks.com
First published in 2023
Hardback ISBN: 979-8-9884339-0-3
Paperback ISBN: 979-8-9884339-1-0
eBook ISBN: 979-8-9884339-2-7

JUVENILE FICTION
/ Social Themes / Friendship & /Emotions & Feelings & /New Experience &
/School & Education & /Animals - Alligators & Crocodiles

One summer day, nestled in a cove among the long marsh reeds, two eggs began to hatch.

Out with a **CRACK!** popped
Alex the Alligator and Chris the Crocodile.

As they rubbed their eyes and stretched they looked up, saw one another, and smiled.

From that day on, Chris and Alex were never apart.
They spent every day together.

They would swim in the rivers,

Play Snap-and-Sneak in the marsh,

And sunbathe on the warm, grassy banks.

At night, they would cuddle up
and read swamp-time stories by
the light of the fireflies.

As Chris and Alex grew and grew so did their friendship.
Before they knew it, they were turning five.

They were excited to be starting Big Chompers school!

But soon they learned they would not be going together.

Alex had to attend Alligator Academy,
the freshwater school for alligators.

And Chris had to go to
Crocodile College,
the saltwater school
for crocodiles.

FRIENDS
DON'T
EAT
FRIENDS

This really made Alex worried.

He couldn't imagine going to school without Chris by his side.

Chris was feeling
scared as well.

What if Alex made so many new friends that he didn't
need him anymore?

Chris found Alex sitting by their favorite fishing hole.

He sat down and said,
"Do you think you'll have more fun playing with other alligators?"

Alex looked shocked and said "Don't be silly, Saltie. No one could replace you. You'll always be my hatch brother."

This made Chris giggle.
"You promise?"
he said, wiping his snout.
"Forever," said Alex.

On the morning of their first day,
Chris handed Alex a gift. "Keep this with you
and think of me," he said, winking.

"I'll see you later, Alligator."

Alex beamed and gave his friend his best brave hug.

"In a while, Crocodile."

That afternoon, Alex sat alone looking glum.
A friendly teacher sat beside him and asked,
"What's wrong, Alex?"

"I miss my friend," Alex said.

"Well, why don't you do something to let
him know you were thinking of him today,"
said the teacher.

Alex looked up excitedly.

He had a great idea!

As the year went on Alex and Chris learned to love their new schools. While Chris had been right and Alex did make many new friends - so did he!

And more friends made playing Swamp-Tag and Chomp Ball so much more fun!

Soon the school year was coming to an end. Chris' Mom and Dad felt that he was now big enough to visit his grandparents for the summer.

Chris was excited.
Especially for all the things his Grandpa
had promised to teach him.

But Alex was not excited. No, not at all.

He stormed off with his arms crossed, pouting. He thought about all the new things Chris would be trying and how he would be left behind.

What if Chris came back and thought all their old games were boring?

Or worse, that Alex was!

When Chris caught up to Alex he said, "Alex,
I didn't tell you the best part." "Hmph," said Alex.

"You know those sneaky bog birds we can never catch?,"
asked Chris. Alex just shrugged.

"My grandpa promised he'd show me his secret trick for
catching them!"

Alex lifted his head and Chris thought he spotted a small smile.
"Alex, you're my best friend. I want to share everything I learn
with you when I get back".

There was a pause and then Alex asked,
"Do you think we could enter
the *Super Snatchers* contest when you come home?"

"Yes!...And win!"
exclaimed Chris,
giving his friend
a high five.

"Cool!" said Alex, feeling better. "Practice hard then."

"I will," said Chris. "I'll see you later, Alligator."

Alex smiled and waved, "In a while, Crocodile."

Stalking Class

When Chris returned he kept his promise.

He taught Alex everything he had learned.

Breath Holding

Lessons in Patience

Leaping Lessons

They became the best bird catchers their swamp had ever seen.

Super Snatchers

Champions!

A few years later, a day came when they learned that things were really going to change. Alex's Dad was going to start a new job chasing airboat tours. Alex's family was moving away.

The two friends were crushed.

As Alex helped his parents pack his art supplies, he suddenly had an idea.

He gathered up a stack of colored paper and markers and ran to find his friend.

"Chris!" he panted. "We can be pen pals!"
"What's a pen pal?" said Chris.
"It's when you send letters or pictures to someone special, telling them what you're up to," Alex told him.

Chris kicked the ground. "That's neat, I guess. But it's not the same as having you around all the time."

"I know," said Alex. "I don't want to leave either. But I know that I'll never forget you."

Chris' eyes watered, but he smiled and said, "We never have before, right?"
"Right," said Alex, with a grin.

"See you later, Alligator."

"In a while, Crocodile."

That summer Alex's family came back to the marsh for a visit. The two friends were together again!

Although they now lived and spent much of their time apart, nothing had changed about the love they felt for their oldest friend...

...and it never would.

Helping Children Manage Separation and Change

Helping our children cope with any kind of separation or big life transition isn't easy. My hope is that, together, you and the child in your life, can use the story of Alex and Chris, along with some of the tips below, to help them manage through some of the difficult feelings and anxieties and come out the other side more resilient and confident!

 **Be a Good Listener-** It is so important to simply open the door on the topic and be a good listener. Versus being the one doing all the talking. Encourage them to be honest and open. That you just want to know how they are feeling without trying to solve everything in the first conversation.

 **Validation of Feelings -** Let them know it's ok to be scared. It's ok to be worried. We all feel that way sometimes. Even grown-ups. Change can be intimidating and it's normal to feel anxious. They need to hear that they are not alone or weak for feeling their feelings.

 **Reassurance and Repetition -** One or two conversations isn't enough. A little check-in each day leading up to a big change to remind and reassure about the love and support that won't be changing even though other things are is key.

 **Out of Sight, But Not Out of Mind -** Come up with mantras, activities, or other ways to stay connected while you're apart. For children, you can suggest that they make a drawing of the family or a happy memory when they are at school and get the "miss yous". Or come up with a mantra they can say to themselves for comfort (Like in "The Kissing Hand" by Audrey Penn). Or think of a special thing for just the two of you to share. A nickname like "hatch brothers" that Alex and Chris used helped to cement their special relationship. Or maybe a secret handshake you can do when you reunite.

 **Memory Object -** Select an item that can bring comfort and a reminder of your connection that they can bring along with them. This could be a friendship bracelet you make together or something like the stuffed animal Chris gave to Alex.

 **Silver Linings -** Talk about the silver linings. While the upcoming change or separation may bring about worries and anxiety, what are the opportunities for good it presents? When Chris and Alex made new friends it made their games even more fun. Visiting grandparents or going to camp or any big trip could teach you new things to bring back with you and share. Talk to your child about what your situation could bring that could be positive.

About the Author
Imogen Shelton

Imogen Shelton lives in Austin, Texas with her husband and her two young boys. Inspiration for "*See You Later Croc-A-Gator*" was two-fold. No stranger to separation herself, Shelton grew up an ocean away from her extended family in the U.K. Then, as a mother, she went through the well-known difficulty of watching her own kids struggle with goodbyes at school drop-off. She is a strong believer that when children can see themselves and their worries reflected in positive stories, the stronger and more resilient they can become. Her hope is that Chris and Alex can teach kids and their families how to better manage change and separation and show that love is enduring despite time and distance apart.

About the Illustrator
Alina Kralia

Alina is a wife and mother of two. While working on "*See You Later Croc-A-Gator*" Alina and her family were transitioning from their home country of the Ukraine to relocate in Germany. This story became close to her heart knowing her boys were feeling similar emotions to Chris as Alex as they dealt with missing their family and friends. Sharing this story helped her family find a way to deal with the separation and begin to believe that their life would be a great journey ahead. Most importantly, it was a reminder that true friends stay with you wherever you go!

www.isheltonbooks.com

Made in the USA
Las Vegas, NV
25 September 2023

78142671R00021